First published in the United States, Great Britain, Canada, Australia, and New Zealand in
2005 by North-South Books, an imprint of NordSüd Verlag AG, Gossau Zürich, Switzerland.
Distributed in the United States by North-South Books Inc., New York.

Library of Congress Cataloging-in-Publication Data is available.
A CIP catalogue record for this book is available from The British Library.
ISBN 0-7358-2031-7 (trade edition) 10 9 8 7 6 5 4 3 2 1
ISBN 0-7358-2032-5 (library edition) 10 9 8 7 6 5 4 3 2 1
Printed in Belgium

Udo Weigelt

Little Donkey's Wish

ILLUSTRATED BY Pirkko Vainio

Translated by Marianne Martens

North-South Books · New York · London

It was a quiet evening in the barn. The only sound was the chomping of the donkeys gathered around the manger, eating their dinner.

"So," said Frederick, the biggest and strongest donkey of them all, "today is Christmas Eve. What do you wish for?"

The donkeys thought for a minute.

"I wish for a nice new summer hat," said Daisy.

"And I wish I could have an extra portion of carrots—every day!" said Max, the fattest of the donkeys. The others laughed.

"I could use a new blanket," said Frederick.

Josie, the youngest and smallest donkey, didn't say anything at all. She was so little that sometimes the others teased her and said that she might not even *be* a real donkey. Most of the time they just ignored her.

But Josie had wishes, too. In fact she had many. One was that she wanted to grow big and strong as fast as possible. Another was that she wished she could pull the farmer's cart all by herself, while the others gazed on in amazement. And she had another secret wish—one that was just as impossible as growing up in a hurry. Josie tucked herself into the corner of her stall. Malina the barn cat snuggled against her legs to comfort her.

Suddenly the barn door opened, and there in the
doorway stood Santa! In a deep voice he wished them
all a good evening.

"One of my reindeeer isn't feeling well," said Santa. "I'm looking for a substitute, and I was wondering if one of you would be willing to help."

Josie's heart beat a little faster. Then she thought, no, Frederick is so strong and Daisy is so fast. Why even Max would probably be a better choice for Santa than I would. Sadly, she hung her head.

The other donkeys were eager to help.

Santa went from one donkey to the next. "You're a fine, strong donkey," he said to Frederick, who proudly lifted his head. "And you must be the fastest donkey of all," he said to Daisy. "And you, Max, I'll bet you could pull two sleighs all by yourself."

Josie hid in the shadows. Santa will just say I'm too small, she thought. He probably won't believe I'm a real donkey either.

Suddenly Malina miaowed, and before Josie could tell her to be quiet, Santa had discovered Josie.

"Aha! Here's another donkey," he said. He looked very large standing there with his hands on his hips. "Hmmmm, I wonder if you'd be willing to help me?"

"Don't you think I'm too small?" Josie asked. "Everybody always tells me I am," she added sadly.

"Well as a matter of fact," said Santa, "I think you're just the right size for the job. But if you're not interested . . ."

"Oh I am!" shouted Josie. She was so excited, she started babbling, "I'd love to help—however I can . . . or however you'll let me . . . or however I should . . . or—"

Santa smiled and led Josie out past the other donkeys, who just stood and stared in disbelief.

When Josie saw how big Santa's sleigh was, her heart sank. The reindeer looked mighty big, too—and so proud.

But in the very back, right in front of the sleigh, there was one reindeer, one who was much smaller than the others. He was so small, that some might think he wasn't even a real reindeer!

Santa hitched Josie in right next to the little reindeer.

"Hello," said the reindeer. "Are you the substitute? Get ready! We're going to go fast!"

"I'll do my best," promised Josie.

Santa cracked his whip, the reindeer started running,
faster and faster, and the sleigh rose high in the air.

Josie didn't even have time to be afraid. She was too
busy working along with the others. She was just as fast
and pulled just as hard as they did.

"You're doing great," the little reindeer said.

They landed on rooftops, where Santa ducked down chimneys. They landed on snow-covered streets and squares. They landed next to a children's hospital, and in front of an orphanage. Everywhere they went Santa distributed presents.

It was all over much too quickly, and soon they were back at Josie's barn again.

Santa unhitched her and led her to her stall. "You were a big help to me, little Josie," he said loudly enough for the other donkeys to hear. "I hope that you will help me again next time I have a sick reindeer."

"Of course I will. Any time!" said Josie.

"So, do you have any Christmas wishes for Santa?"

Josie thought for a minute. Then she said, "I wish for a new hat for Daisy, a nice blanket for Frederick, and for Max, extra carrots—every day."

Santa laughed. "Nothing for yourself, Josie?" he asked.

"Oh, tonight I got my secret wish," Josie replied. "I flew with Santa Claus!"